The Sea Wolf

Jack London

8472
F
FAG

ILLUSTRATED

Pendulum Press, Inc.

West Haven, Connecticut

ISBN 0-88301-093-3 Complete Set
     0-88301-322-3 Paperback
     0-88301-334-7 Hardcover

Library of Congress Catalog Number 78-51553

Published by
Pendulum Press, Inc.
An Academic Industries, Inc. Company
The Academic Building
Saw Mill Road
West Haven, Connecticut   06516

Printed in the United States of America

to the teacher

Pendulum Press is proud to offer the NOW AGE ILLUSTRATED Series to schools throughout the country. This completely new series has been prepared by the finest artists and illustrators from around the world. The script adaptations have been prepared by professional writers and revised by qualified reading consultants.

Implicit in the development of the Series are several assumptions. Within the limits of propriety, anything a child reads and/or wants to read is *per se* an educational tool. Educators have long recognized this and have clamored for materials that incorporate this premise. The sustained popularity of the illustrated format, for example, has been documented, but it has not been fully utilized for educational purposes. Out of this realization, the NOW AGE ILLUSTRATED Series evolved.

In the actual reading process, the illustrated panel encourages and supports the student's desire to read printed words. The combination of words and picture helps the student to a greater understanding of the subject; and understanding, that comes from reading, creates the desire for more reading.

The final assumption is that reading as an end in itself is self-defeating. Children are motivated to read material that satisfies their quest for knowledge and understanding of their world. In this Series, they are exposed to some of the greatest stories, authors, and characters in the English language. The Series will stimulate their desire to read the original edition when their reading skills are sufficiently developed. More importantly, reading books in the NOW AGE ILLUS-TRATED Series will help students establish a mental "pegboard" of information — images, names, and concepts — to which they are exposed. Let's assume, for example, that a child sees a television commercial which features Huck Finn in some way. If he has read the NOW AGE Huck Finn, the TV reference has meaning for him which gives the child a surge of satisfaction and accomplishment.

After using the NOW AGE ILLUSTRATED editions, we know that you will share our enthusiasm about the Series and its concept.

—The Editors

about the author

Jack London, who was to become one of the most highly paid authors of his day, was born in 1876 in San Francisco. He was the tenth child in his family, and consequently grew up in poverty. He had to work long hours for little pay; and he fell into the hands of thieves and cutthroats at an early age. In a few years he turned to drinking as a solace for his troubles.

Fortunately, before he was ruined by alcohol, London set sail on a seal ship. By the time he returned to San Francisco, many of his former companions had died. After a brief stint with the railway, London succumbed to his great desire to travel. He spent considerable time in the Klondike region of Alaska, which provided him with a setting for *The Call of the Wild*. Here, too, London encountered the dog after which he modelled his hero, Buck.

In *The Sea Wolf* London tells the story of a lonely man who struggles with the animal and human natures within him. Many critics have suggested that Wolf Larsen, the captain, must have been in some ways very much like London himself.

*a boat that takes people back and forth across narrow spans of water

*two high cliffs on either side of San Francisco Bay

I remember pulling down life jackets from racks while the red-faced man put them on the women.

They were like rats in a trap and all they could do was scream.

A cry arose that we were sinking. I was pushed over the side.

The water was cold. It bit like the grip of death. All around I could hear people screaming.

The ship shot by, and I caught sight of a man smoking a cigar. I could see the smoke coming from his lips as he slowly turned and looked my way.

It was a chance thing, but life and death were in that look. Yet he did see me, for suddenly he sprang to the wheel.

I passed out again, but awoke in a ship's galley.*

That'll do, Yonson. Can't you see you've nearly rubbed his skin off?

*kitchen

When I stepped onto the deck the fog was gone and the sun sparkled on the water. No land was in sight, but a long way off I could see some ships' sails coming closer.

Soon my attention was drawn back to the ship I was on. As I drew near a crowd of sailors, I caught sight of a man lying on the deck.

Just then the dying man's head rolled to the side. His mouth froze into a grin at the world he had just left.

Suddenly the captain began to shout. From what I could understand, it seemed that the mate* had drunk too much in San Francisco and then had died. This left the captain with one man too few on his ship.

*the man next in rank to the captain of a ship

I wish to be brought safely to land. Of course I will pay you well.

And I have a different idea for the good of your soul. My mate's gone, so a sailor takes his place and the cabin boy* takes the sailor's place. You, my friend, become the cabin boy for twenty dollars a month.

Meanwhile, the ship I'd seen before was about to pass us by.

Is that ship going to San Francisco? Will you signal her to pick me up?

Aye, she is, but I've lost my signal book overboard.

One thousand dollars if you take me to land!

Ahoy!**

Don't mind this man. He is out of his mind!

*a very young sailor who serves meals and runs errands on a ship
**hello

The sailors were mostly English and Scandinavian* and their faces seemed heavy and worn from drink. The seal hunters, on the other hand, had stronger faces.

Wolf Larsen's face was not heavy. Nor did it have the harsh lines the seal hunters' faces had. Yet he could surely handle a ship, and the men on it as well.

But the cook was another matter. Now that I was working for him, he began to make things hard for me.

You'll call me Mr. Mugridge now. And what's your name?

Humphrey Van Weyden.

I knew little about peeling potatoes and washing greasy pots so I wasn't much help in the kitchen. This made the cook very angry.

*from Sweden, Norway, or Denmark

That first day I learned a lot about a heavy sea.

You there, Van. Grab hold of something!

Serve you bloody well right if your neck was broken!

That "lesson" gave me a sore knee that bothered me for months.

You may be a little sore, but you're learning to walk on a ship. You're getting your "sea legs."

That night I lay in pain in my bunk. I thought sadly about how I, Humphrey Van Weyden, a gentleman, was now a lowly cabin boy.

The next morning, however, I was given the mate's tiny cabin. The new mate was sent to a bunk.

Later I went to Wolf's cabin to make the bed and was greatly surprised. It was clear that he was a learned man.

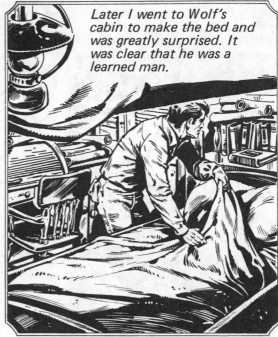

But when I happened to toss some ashes overboard into the wind . . .

. . . he kicked me. I was stunned, wondering how anyone could have two sides so different from one another.

Every day I learned a little more about the captain. The men were preparing boats for a seal hunt, and they talked while they worked.

I found that Wolf Larsen was not very well-liked among sealing captains. Every sailor seemed to have some excuse for being on the Ghost.

And many said that the hunters were all men who could not sign aboard any decent ship.

The *Ghost* will really be a ghost ship with more dead men on board before this trip is over. Wolf Larsen is a beast. 'Tis no heart he has at all.

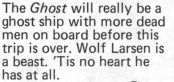

Take Johnson there, he's a fine sailor. But it's to trouble he'll come with Wolf as sure as sparks rise into the air.

Wolf is strong and Johnson is strong. But it's the way of a wolf to hate the strong, and that's what he'll see in Johnson.

That afternoon a young sailor was sent to climb one of the masts.* On the rigging** he froze from fear, and was not able to move. His life was in great danger.

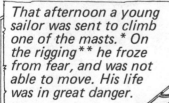

I'll bet he can't eat his supper.

*a tall pole that holds up one or more sails

**the rope nets that men climb to reach one of the ship's sails

Evening came and I went to set the table and serve dinner. Later, while making an extra trip, I saw the boy who had been in the rigging. He was walking weakly across the deck.

Later, Wolf stopped in the galley.

You were looking sick this afternoon.

It was because of the way you treated that boy.

The way you felt is like being seasick. Some people get seasick, and some don't.

Don't you place any value on life at all?

Why, life is the cheapest thing in the world. There is only so much water, so much earth, so much air. But life goes on and on.

The days passed. I stole odd moments to gaze at the beauty of the sea and sky. Then one morning the captain came up to me singing.

"Oh, I am the wind the seamen love,
I am steady and strong and true;
They follow my track by the clouds above,
O'er the fathomless* tropic blue."

I looked into his face. It was glowing like the stars, but I threw his own words back at him.

Ah, I cannot get you to understand. Of course life is without value—except to itself.

"Life is a cheap thing and without value."

Sometimes I thought Wolf Larsen was mad, or half mad at least. Other times I took him for a great man. But I never could understand him!

*never-ending, never understood

A couple of sailors were called to take the cook on deck and give him some air.

The money you have won is mine, sir.

"Was mine" you should have said, not "is mine."

It is not a question of words, but of what is right and wrong.

It was about a minute before he spoke. When he did, he sounded sad.

This is the first time I have heard someone talk about right and wrong on this ship. At one time I dreamed I might someday talk with men about such things.

Then we began to talk about many things. I was surprised that he knew so much.

Time passed. Supper was nearly ready, and when Thomas Mugridge showed up looking angry, I prepared to go. But Wolf stopped me.

Cooky, you'll have to work by yourself tonight. I'm busy with Van, so do the best you can without him.

And so I had three days of rest doing nothing but talking with Wolf Larsen. Thomas Mugridge growled a lot and did my work as well as his own.

It was a rest which I knew would bring me trouble.

Watch out for squalls.* Just when you're thinking you know that man, he'll turn around and rip your sails to rags.

My friend was right. That night when I spoke to Wolf about the things he believed in, he flew into a rage. It was a mad wolf in him.

The cook let me know I'd pay dearly for the days I was off.

Too afraid to strike me, he spent every free moment sharpening knives and grumbling to himself.

*sudden strong storms of rain and wind

Day after day this went on. At last I could stand no more.

I stole five cans of milk from the galley and traded them to a sailor for a knife.

The next morning when Mugridge pulled out his knife . . .

I pulled out mine.

For two hours we sat like madmen staring at each other. Neither of us wanted to fight. Then the cook spoke.

You're not so bad, Van. You've got nerve and I like you in a way. So come on and shake hands.

Afraid though I was, I was less afraid than he. I had won. I refused to shake his hand.

Come on, Van.

Cooky's finished. Van runs the galley now.

My friendship with Wolf grew, yet I was nothing to him but a toy. As long as I pleased him, all went well. But if I made him angry, I was sent back to the galley.

Were he not so terrible a man, I could almost feel sorry for him when things went wrong.

Oh, my head. My head!

For three days his blinding headache lasted. He suffered like a wild animal.

Some days later he showed me a system* he was inventing to make guiding a ship much easier.

Why haven't you done great things in this world?

Van, do you know the parable** of the sower who went out to sow his grain? You will remember that some of the seeds grew up among thorns and that the thorns choked them.

Well?

Well? It was not well. I was one of those seeds. My parents were poor people who sowed their sons on the waves. There is no more to tell . . .

*method; way of doing something
**fable; story

And, Van, I can tell you that you know more about me than any living man except my own brother.

And where is *he*?

He is master of the steamship *Macedonia*. We'll meet him off the coast of Japan. Men call him "Death Larsen."

The sailors and hunters seemed to know a little about Wolf Larsen's brother. They talked about him as if he were a wild man.

On *Wolf and Death Larsen*, Louis had these words:

Aye, watch out for squalls when the two of them meet. They hate each other like the wolf pups they both are.

Meanwhile the Ghost was turning into a devil's ship with fights every day among the men.

When the season's over, you may kill and eat each other for all I care. But not now.

I think even the hunters were surprised at what the captain had said. As wicked as they were, they were certainly afraid of him.

For when Johnson spoke out against the harsh things Wolf often did, he was dragged to the cabin and beaten by Wolf and the mate.

He's a better man than you are. He stands up for what he believes.

Quite true, Van, but even a living insect is better than a dead man.

Then there was trouble in the fore-castle,* and it could be seen every day in the faces of the sailors.

Next, two of the hunters shot each other. When he heard of it, Wolf stormed in and beat them both up.

You stupid men! I'd kill you if I didn't need you.

It was like living in a terrible dream.

*part of a ship in which the crew lives

Wolf gave me a lamp and ordered me to follow him. In the forecastle, Wolf moved among the sleeping sailors. As he went, he checked their pulses* to see who was really awake.

When we got to Johnson's bunk there was trouble.

There must have been several sailors who had wanted to kill the mate and the captain, for suddenly the forecastle was like a hive of angry bees.

Somehow Wolf Larsen got away from the sailors who wanted to kill him.

*the pounding of blood that can be felt at a person's wrist

For several minutes the place remained dark. I heard men moaning. Then someone lit the lantern.

How'd he get away?

He's the devil himself.

Then a lamp shone at the top of the ladder and a hunter called down to the men.

Hey Van! the old man wants you.

I jumped for the ladder.

You little rat!

Easy man, Van's all right.

I'll say I haven't seen or heard a thing!

Wolf was waiting in his cabin.

Get to work, doctor. If I had any good words at all, I would tell you that I am deeply grateful to have you here.

I cleaned his wounds as he spoke.

You're a handy man, Van. Since now we're short a captain's mate, I'm giving you the job. You'll be called Mr. Van Weyden from now on.

No! I won't be mate on this devil's ship. Besides, I don't know enough.

Wolf Larsen's face grew hard, but his eyes shone like a bad boy's.

You know enough. And now, good night, Mr. Van Weyden.

Good night, Mr. Larsen.

At least I no longer had to wash dishes.

The wind's shifted, Mr. Van Weyden. Go on deck and turn the ship around.

I would go on deck, call my friend Louis, and learn from him what was to be done. Then I'd give the orders to the crew.

Here I was, a landlubber,* second in command. But the sailors helped me and I was secretly proud of myself.

For the sailors, however, life got worse. Wolf spent all his time trying to make their lives unpleasant.

Faster, you lazy pig!

Leach, a friend of Johnson's, fought with Wolf again and again.

Wolf only laughed and seemed to enjoy it.

Leach and Johnson would have killed Wolf at the first chance. But that chance never came.

*someone who likes to stay on land, not on the sea

You are a coward to treat men this way when you are so much stronger than they are.

You're the real coward. You believe they're right, but you won't help them. You are afraid, and you want to live.

At last we neared the coast of Japan. There we found the great seal herd heading north.

We slaughtered* the seals and threw the meat to the sharks. We kept the hides, which would one day be made into clothes for the vain** women in our cities.

On some days, we hunted with other sealing ships.

*killed in large numbers
**having too much love for oneself

And more than once we faced terrible storms.

Sometimes the storms rose so quickly that our small boats had to be taken aboard other ships. Then we would have to search for them.

But more than the storms, we feared the sea fogs that fell on us like blankets.

During this time, Wolf Larsen was again and again kept below by his terrible headaches. That gave me a chance to learn more about navigation. *

*the art of keeping a ship on its course

One day Leach came to see me.

How could a person get to Japan from here?

I was very happy to tell him. He wanted to try to escape.

The next morning, he and Johnson were gone in one of the small boats. Wolf was angry. While he paced the deck, we looked for the missing crew.

On the third day a boat was sighted. My heart sank, but Wolf's eyes gleamed with victory!

Yet we were all in for a surprise.

May I never shoot another seal again if that isn't a woman!

Wolf ordered me to take the lady below where she would be safe.

The sailors said we're close to Japan and that you'd have us there by tonight.

Our captain is a strange man. I beg you to be ready for anything.

But I thought shipwrecked people were always shown every kindness.

This man is cruel and evil. But trust me, and I will try to help you.

Then she fell asleep and I went back on deck. I found that a gale* was blowing.

Suddenly, I saw Leach and Johnson. Wolf saw them too.

Give them a chance!

I promise I won't lay a hand on them.

*a very strong wind

We soon caught up with them. Johnson's face was worn and tired. I waved and he answered, but his wave was hopeless. He seemed to be saying good-bye.

Soon our ship had passed their little boat. For hours Wolf made fun of them, for they were still nearby.

So you've changed your minds and want to come aboard. Well, then, just keep coming!

The storm grew worse, until at last a great wave cap- sized* them.

Pity about that! But they only got what they deserved, and I never laid a hand on them. Be- sides, I've got four new sailors aboard to take their places.

And saying this, he set our course north, away from the coast.

*turned over their boat

The next day, our boats were out sealing when black smoke appeared on the horizon. *

I'll bet it's the *Macedonia*. When you and your brother get together, there is always trouble.

As if in answer, the Macedonia *steamed by and dropped her fourteen boats in front of ours. The line of boats, like a huge broom, swept the seal herd before it. The hunting was spoiled for us.*

One by one Wolf called in our boats and gave secret orders.

He means to get even.

Sure enough, when the Macedonia *sailed over the horizon, we passed our own boats and headed toward hers.*

*the point where the sea and sky seem to meet

There may be blood. Won't you go below, Miss Brewster?

I may be a woman, but I'm as brave as you, Captain Larsen.

Books, brains and bravery. You'd make a good wife for a pirate chief.

Within minutes, we'd captured* five of Death Larsen's boats. We had our own boats back on board as well.

Look, the *Macedonia* is returning!

Yes, and I'll beat you yet, brother!

The Macedonia, *throwing out black smoke, was bearing down on us. But we set sails, and the* Ghost *headed for a nearby fog bank.*

*caught

One moment there was clear sky overhead and the next we were lost in thick fog.

I'd sure like to hear my brother now! Take the wheel, Mr. Van Weyden. We won't stay around here tonight.

Wolf left to pass out whiskey and to make peace with the men he had captured. He had not had any headaches for weeks. When I went below, I found him in high spirits.

Won't Death's men try to escape?

I'm going to pay my hunters for every seal shot by this new bunch. There won't be any escaping if my men can help it.

I'll take the wheel, and call you to take over at midnight. You'd better get some sleep now.

I did as he said. As I went to bed, I could hear the cries of the sailors. I noticed that Wolf, however, drank nothing at all.

Later, I was awakened suddenly. Rushing to the door, I saw poor Maud fighting to get away from Wolf Larsen.

I had my knife in my hand. But suddenly Wolf fell back.

I'm sick! Van Weyden, where are you? Get me to my cabin!

Is there anything I can do?

No, it's these headaches again. Leave me alone until morning.

Now may be our only chance. We must act at once!

There was no one on deck. Quickly we loaded food and blankets into one of the boats and made our escape.

There lies Japan!

Humphrey Van Weyden, you are a brave man.

For many days we drifted wherever the wind and sea took us.

But the wind we hoped would take us to Japan was blowing us out to sea instead. Free of Wolf Larsen, however, I was no longer afraid of dying at sea.

Finally, one morning . . .

Look, land!

I began to love Maud more each day. She needed me, and that made me strong.

Soon we were safe ashore.

I unloaded the boat and began to make camp.

There was no one else living on the island. Winter was coming, and we needed a place to live. So we set about building a stone hut. *

Before too many weeks passed, we were well prepared to spend the winter. Our hut was warm and dry.

Do you feel safe?

Yes, but I have a strange feeling that something is going to happen.

*a small house

The next morning when I stepped outside, I was stopped short by what I saw. It was the *Ghost*, its sails down, lying just off shore.

Before Maud awoke I decided to look around the ship. On deck I discovered that the boats were all missing. It looked like the men had left the forecastle in a hurry.

Suddenly, a noise made me turn around. There was Wolf, alone and without a gun. Now was my chance to kill him, but I couldn't pull the trigger.

You're weak. You can't kill me like a snake because I have hands and feet, and a body like yours. Bah! I had hoped for better things of you, Van.

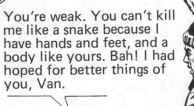

He called me by name. Yet somehow I knew he was now blind.

What happened?

That brother of mine got me—offered the crew more money, and they went with him. But the worst thing is these headaches—they'll finish me soon enough.

Just then an attack struck him, and I returned to shore.

All those head-aches—perhaps he is very ill and dying.

But his spirit is still strong. If we repair the ship, we can return to the world.

We began work at once.

But our work angered the wolf . . .

Don't you mess with my ship! I plan on dying here.

Well *we* don't! I couldn't shoot you before, but I *will* shoot you now if you try anything.

Repairing the ship was hard work. But with Maud's help everything went well.

For days we worked, but then one morning . . .

Oh, Humphrey!

We must begin again.

Wolf, though blind, had torn apart what we had done and had let the masts and spars* drift out to sea.

Although our spirits were low, we went back to work. Luckily, we were able to save the masts.

The work went on, but now we kept watch at night.

One day Wolf had one of his headache attacks while we were working.

*poles that hold up part of a ship's sail

When I bent to help him, his hand grabbed me like a steel trap.

I screamed, and Maud came running. She bravely knocked Wolf senseless.

Now that he is helpless, we'll keep him that way. From now on we will live in the cabin, and Wolf will live here.

The sickness has gone to my brain. I cannot see, and soon I won't be able to speak. All the time I will be alive, and yet powerless.*

The terrible old Wolf Larsen was still there. But now he was trapped inside his own body.

*not able to act

Some days later, speech left him. For a while, however, he could still write.

My mind is still working. Like a wise man, I think about life and death . . .

And immortality?*

He tried to write, but three times the pencil fell from his fingers.

BOSH**

It was his last message.

After many weeks, our hard work was finished. The ship was ready.

There was a wild, happy look in Maud's eyes as we escaped into safe water.

*life that does not end; life after death
**a word that means "rubbish" or "I don't believe it"

The Ghost *sailed well, but some days later we met a terrible storm.*

When it passed, Maud called me below.

He died during the storm.

Now he is free from himself.

The next morning after breakfast we brought Wolf's body on deck and prepared to bury it.

I remember only one part of the service— "And the body shall be cast into the sea . . ."

Maud looked at me, surprised and shocked. But I was remembering something I had seen before. I had to bury Wolf as I had seen Wolf bury another man.

The body, wrapped in a sack, slipped feet first into the sea. The iron dragged it down, and it was gone.

Goodbye, Wolf.

Just then I caught a clear view of a ship sailing toward us. It was a United States revenue cutter.*

Look! We are saved!

I hardly know whether to be glad or not.

*a small armed boat used by the Coast Guard

words to know

horizon	vain	pulses	squalls
capsized	navigation	forecastle	fathomless
gale	powerless	system	galley

questions

1. How did Humphrey Van Weyden happen to be aboard the *Ghost*, Wolf Larsen's ship?

2. From what the cook says to Humphrey at the bottom of page 13, can you tell why Humphrey began to dislike him from the very beginning?

3. Compare Wolf Larsen's beliefs about life (on page 21) with your own. Do you believe that a man's whole life depends on luck and violence?

4. Wolf was a hard, mean man, but he had some good points. Name at least three things that were good about him.

5. How did Humphrey finally stand up to the cook and refuse to take any more bad treatment from him? What was the result?

6. What were the sailors like who worked on Wolf's ship? Prove your answer by giving examples from the story.

7. How did Humphrey, or Van as the captain called him, become the ship's mate? How did he feel about his promotion?

8. What happened to Wolf at the end of the story? What happened to Humphrey and Maud Brewster?